Expressions of the mind in words

Writings by a 9 year old kid

Lakshyajay kalita

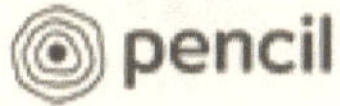

ISBN 978-93-5458-328-5

Published in India 2021 by Pencil

A brand of
One Point Six Technologies Pvt. Ltd.
123, Building J2, Shram Seva Premises,
Wadala Truck Terminal, Wadala (E)
Mumbai 400037, Maharashtra, INDIA
E connect@thepencilapp.com
W www.thepencilapp.com

Author biography

Master Lakshyajay Kalita came to our lives on August 30, 2010. He was born in Itanagar, Arunachal Pradesh at Ramakrishna Mission Hospital. Even during his early childhood, he started showing interest in books. He was quite different from other children and never cried or created any ruckus for toys. As parents, we never got a chance to scold him or shout at him. He had a very close relation with his paternal grandmother, and there are many incidents, which proved that he had a telepathic connection with her.

Lakshyajay started his schooling in Sri Sri Ravishankar Vidya Mandir, Itanagar. It was during this period that his headmistress Mrs. Sushmita Shome realized his potential and Lakshyajay made his first public speech in the school Annual day program when he was just in Class LKG. Lakshyajay is an avid book reader and has a small library of his own.

Apart from reading books, which is his favourite hobby, Lakshyajay has immense love for Nature and has a creative mind. He is a good classical singer and has cleared Madhyama in Vocal Music from Bhatkhande University. He has also performed stage performances in the Guwahati District library twice on the convocation ceremony of Sarbabharatiya Sangeet O Sanskriti Parishad, Kolkata. He has also earned prize in the All India Talent Search Examination conducted by Sarbabharatiya Sangeet O Sanskriti Parishad, Kolkata. He has also rendered a Malayalam song on the occasion of Onam Festival in Itanagar.

Lakshyajay has had the privilege of meeting great classical Maestros namely, Pandit Ajay Chakraborty, Oddissi danseur Smt. Nandini Ghosal and Pakhawaj artiste Sri Kishore Ghose while on his trips to Kolkata.

Lakshyajay believes that books are his best friends and wherever he goes he makes sure that a book always remains with him. He loves writing stories and remains engrossed in his own thoughts throughout the day. His ambition is to become a very good human being, a writer for a good cause and an IAS officer.

CONTENTS

Foreword

In this age of technology, it is common to see children remaining engrossed in TVs, Mobile phones, gaming stations etc. Even books have become online. Lack of family time, the race towards earning more and more wealth has alienated our children from their natural life.

However, Lakshyajay decided to remain aloof from the hazards of Technologies and decided to make books his best friends from an early age. Maybe it was due to the fact, that his grandfathers, his maternal grandmother, his father and mother were also avid book lovers. His parents decision to gift him books instead of toys maybe created a love for books in his heart.

Another motivating force behind his inclination towards books and writing is the inspiration and encouragement he got from Mrs. Sushmita Shome, Principal of his first school, Sri Sri Ravi Shankar Vidya Mandir, Itanagar, whom he called Madam Jyethai. It was she who realized his potential and made him make his first public appearance by giving a speech on Dr. APJ Abdul Kalam when he was in Class LKG.

Reading books made his young mind creative and he started penning down his thoughts right form Class I. It was in Class I when his first writing was published,

courtesy the BRIDGE, an Annual Souvenir of OLD BOYS ASSOCIATION SAINIK SCHOOL GOALPARA. And that was the start.

With a view to keep his creativity alive and to preserve the various thoughts of his mind, it was his mother who had a desire to publish a book on his 10th Birthday. This desire has led to the publication of this book, which is titled "Expressions of the mind". Our heartfelt thanks to the special people and well-wishers for sending us the words of blessings, without which Lakshyajay could not have achieved what he has till now. The writings selected here are the ones, which we feel, are the best amongst his numerous writings until now. No corrections have been made to the contents in the book, as it was our endeavour to print the books as it has been written by him. Hence there are chances of some grammatical errors in the book.

Introduction

I dedicate this book as a loving tribute to my dearest grandmother, Late Mrs. Anjali Kalita, with whom I shared a very special connection. She was an exceptional and beautiful lady, a lady who loved reading books and encouraged us to do what we wanted. My Aaitaa was a very popular lady, who spread happiness and laughter around her.

I still wonder why you left us so early Aaitaa, depriving us from your love and affection. My memories of you are very limited, but I remember you as my best friend, my most loved person. I am yet to see another lady as beautiful as you.
I know you would have been the happiest person today on seeing this effort of mine. I believe and know that you must be happy wherever you are and showering your blessings on all of us.

You will always remain in my heart and continue to provide me the inspiration I need.
Love you Aaitaa.

Jumon (Lakshyajay Kalita)

Blessings from Lakshyajay's Maternal grandfather, Sri Munindra Nath Tamuly.

To put it in a nutshell, I am going to express about my first grandson (Jumon) Sri Lakshyajay Kalita. It is known that he could read English from Class KG. From a very early age, he developed an interest in reading books. He spent his time reading books. He did not have interest in mobile phones. Now he is in Class IV and can read all kind of books rapidly.

Now we feel that that he is a God gifted child. May God always bless him. He also knows music and acting. He is the pearl of our eyes (Sokur Moni).

I wish him the best of luck on his 10th Birthday, which falls on August 30, 2020

Blessings message from The Former Principal of Sainik School Goalpara, the person who made an impact in the life of Lakshyajay.

My heartfelt wishes and compliments to Master Lakshyajay Kalita on turning 10 years on 30 Aug 2020. Every birthday is a milestone and every milestone provides a cumulative picture of the growth that has taken place in a young mind.

I met Laksh in Feb 2017, when his family visited Sainik School Goalpara, Assam. I was quite impressed with his inquisitive nature and intelligent approach towards things. He was a promising young boy, a bundle of energy, loaded with talents and all the good things childhood and good parents could offer. Over the years, I have seen him mature into a versatile boy with varied interests in many fields.

Every spark needs to be ignited to grow into a flame. His parents' initiative to celebrate and encourage his creative talents in the form of a book on his 10th birthday is praiseworthy. I wish Laksh happiness on his birthday and am sure all of us would see him achieve many milestones in his creative endeavours.

Warm regards and best wishes on this special occasion.

Edwin JothiRajan

17 Jul 2020 **Captain, Indian Navy**

A MESSAGE OF BLESSINGS FROM Mrs. SUSHMITA SHOME, FORMER HEADMISTRESS OF LAKSHYAJAY'S FIRST SCHOOL, SRI SRI RAVI SHANKAR VIDYA MANDIR, ITANAGAR.

Lakshyajay Kalita was a student of SSRVM. He was a very talented student. When he was in class LKG he could read English and Hindi book of class V fluently. At the age of 5, he delivered a speech on Dr Abdul Kalam and won appreciation from the distinguished guests present there on the occasion of our annual day programme. He loved stories that had happy endings. Sometimes he would make own stories with good and happy ending.

He was also interested in singing. I never saw him fighting or quarreling with anyone.

He is a child with certain god-gifted qualities.

I wish him all success in life. I wish his hidden talents gets manifested with proper guidance and encouragement

A MESSAGE OF BLESSINGS FROM Mrs. MARAMI SAIKIA BARUAH, HEADMISTRESS OF LAKSHYAJAY'S PRESENT SCHOOL, TEZPUR GURUKUL.

Hello Everyone

It is my esteemed privilege to write about this supremely talented boy. I take this opportunity to wish all the best and success to the author of "Expressions of mind in words" at such a young age. I genuinely appreciate his dedication in writing. At some point I feel awestruck to his talent. May Almighty bless him for a bright future, where he is just a new entrant to reach the globe.

Hope everyone will encourage him in a great length.

MY SWEET MOMENTS WITH GRANDMA, MY AAITAA

(A Tribute to his grandmother, who left for her heavenly abode when he was just 4 years old. He had a very special bonding with his Aita. On her 5th Death Anniversary, he decided to pen down the various incidents he heard from us.)

I want to share some sweet moments I had with my Grandma, whom I called Aaitaa. My Aaitaa's name is Anjali Kalita. Many of the moments I am sharing are what I heard from my parents, my grandfather.

When I was one month old, I went to my Aaitaa's home in Jamugurihat for the first time. When it was time for us to return to Itanagar, Aaitaa said to me, O my sweetheart you will leave me and go away, and I

started sobbing very loudly. I don't know how I could understand her at the age of just one month. But when I cried, Aaitaa also cried and even my parents also cried.

During festivals, we always visited Aaitaa. Sometimes my cousins Loyona (manuba) and Neelarnav (bumon dada) also used to visit Jamuguri. We played a lot and Aaitaa loved to see us playing. My Aaitaa created a pattern in giving our nicknames. My father's nickname is Dumon; she named my cousin Neelarnav as Bumon, me as Jumon. See, our nicknames follow a pattern.

My Aaitaa had a pet dog named Tom. One day Tom was very sick and Aaitaa was very sad. Meanwhile in Itanagar, I started crying, saying I wanted to visit Aaitaa. We came down to Jamuguri and then Tom died. We buried him. Aaitaa was very happy that we were with her when she was sad. And not only that time, but everytime, whenever my Aaitaa was sick or sad, I used to cry in Itanagar and force my parents to come near Aaitaa. Once when Aaitaa cut her finger very badly, I forced my parents to come to Jamuguri and on seeing us, Aaitaa was really surprised as she was not able to cook food. I really don't know how, but it really happened. My dad says that was telepathy.

After Tom died, Aaitaa brought another puppy named as Poppy. I played many games with Aaitaa. When I was very little, Aaitaa used to close down the buttons

of my shirt and I used to yell "yaaaaa" and open the shirt. And when I used to lie in bed, Aaitaa used to put a blanket on me and I would kick it off. These were some games Aaitaa loved playing with me. Whenever we used to visit Aaitaa's home or she used to visit our home, I always used to sleep with mom and Aaitaa.

During my mom's operation, when I was only two years old, I slept the whole day in my Aaitaa's lap. Aaitaa was an interesting lady. Even though she was an Aaitaa, she didn't like anyone calling her old. She was not like other Aaitaas. She was modern just like me. Her hobbies were singing, travelling, reading books etc. She loved eating pizzas, ice cream, pulao, biryani, just like me. Whenever Aaitaa visited us in Itanagar, we used to go to Parks, where she played on the swing. We used to visit restaurants and have lots of fun. She was a very beautiful lady, the most beautiful lady on earth. Every month we used to visit Aaitaa.

But the saddest part is that, Aaitaa left us five years ago and left for her heavenly abode. I could just get her company for 4 years. Now there is another cousin who was born after Aaitaa passed away. He is one year old. His name is Medhansh, but following Aita's pattern, we call him Sumon. Now Poppy, Aaitaa's pet dog has a litter of pups and some of them have even grown up. After Aaitaa's death, we do not visit Jamuguri very often. Aaitaa's home becomes desolate without her presence. Everyone has a Grandma

(Aaitaa), but my Aaitaa is the best. I miss you a lot Aaitaa and I love you.

THE FIRST STORY THE PYTHON

Every new venture has a beginning. Lakshyajay's first step towards penning down his thoughts started when he was in Class I. With his tiny hands which were usually used to just writing words, he started framing sentences on his own. It was the time for our School OBA Meet, and we required write-ups for our Magazine. Just to give a try we asked him to write a story, which Lakshyajay penned down instantaneously for our magazine named BRIDGE.

And the editor of BRIDGE was kind enough to consent for publishing his story without making any corrections. We remain indebted to the Sainik School Goalpara Old Boys Association for acting as the stepping-stone for our son to venture out to a new world.

The story is being published exactly as he has written it. No corrections have been made, as we wanted to preserve it as the way he wrote. When he reads the story today, he feels awkward, but this story is very precious as this was the foundation stone for his writing journey

"Once upon a time, a python was hungry. A man see the tree, he is climbed the tree. The python is very happy, he said, wow, my lunch is ready. The man go to the treetop, the python see the man with dangerous eyes. The man said, oh no, this is a python. The man is very scared. The python eat the man. The python is very happy and go to other tree to wait for his next lunch.

Moral: if you are wait, you are great"

IT HAPPENED TO ME- EPISODE I
(The friendly dog)

(The incident where a dog proved that it can be great partner and only wants to be a true friend)

One day I, along with my parents went to my uncle's home. I saw a big dog in his home. The dog suddenly jumped on me, and I got scared a little. My dad told me not to get scared, as it was just trying to play with me. But I still was scared and thought that it wanted to attack me.

I went to my uncle's library. It has lots of books. I am a book lover. I choose some books for me. Some I brought home and some I read in my uncle's home, while Mom and Dad was busy in talking.

Then we had lunch. After taking lunch, we started walking around the village. It was a nice village with lots of tress and ponds too. I saw fungus on the water. Uncle has a pond in his home. We went to the pond in my uncle's home. Uncle threw fishes' food in the pond. I played with the fishes. I saw golden and black fishes.

After playing with the fishes, we came inside and I was reading comics. The dog, of which I was scared, picked up my sandal in his mouth and gave it to me. I was surprised and said to my parents that the dog was giving me a gift. We all had a good laugh.

Then we drove back home. When we were in the car, the dog started barking loudly as he wanted to come with us. I felt bad to leave my new friend, whom I was scared of in the beginning, but he proved that he just wanted to play with me.

FRIENDLY TIM

(The writer himself is afraid of dogs... Maybe this is how he wants to get rid of his fears!)

One day a boy named Rahul went to his uncle's home with his parents. His uncle's name was Rohit. "Uncle" said Rahul, "how are you"? "I am fine" replied uncle Rohit. Rahul saw his cousin Ishant. "We have got a new dog," said Ishant. "Its name is Tim. Do you want to see it?" Rahul was afraid of dogs. So he said, "Ishant, you know my biggest fear is dog. Can we play something like cricket?"

However, it was too late. Ishant brought Tim out. Tim licked Rahul playfully and tried to jump on him. Rahul ran in fear. Tim chased Rahul. Rahul jumped over a fence and so did Tim. "Save me" cried Rahul. "Help!" Rahul tripped over a stone and fell down. Uncle Rohit came and stopped Tim. " Don't let that dog come near me" said Rahul, who was angry with Tim. Ishant said, "He was just playing with you, Rahul". Uncle Rohit took Rahul home. After some time Rahul went to sleep after playing with Ishant.

The next day Rahul asked his parents if he and Ishant

could go to the bank of the river and have their lunch there. His parents asked him to talk to Ishant. “If he agrees to go, I will make you some sandwiches,” his mother said. Rahul asked Ishant. “Only if Tim comes with us, I will go,” said Ishant. Rahul said, “Oh come on, let’s leave that dog alone”. Ishant said, “As you wish, but I will not go without Tim”. “Ok Tim can come but don’t let him come near me”, said Rahul.

They went to the bank of the river with some sandwiches, which Mom made. They played there. Some hours later Rahul went unknowingly very close to the water. “Watch out!” Shouted Ishant. But it was too late. Rahul fell down into the river. He shouted for help. But how could little Ishant save him? Tim jumped into the river, caught Rahul by his collar, and tried pulling him to the bank. Ishant rushed home and told uncle Rohit what happened.

Rohit rushed to the bank of the river with Rahul’s parents and saw that Tim had already pulled Rahul out of the river. Rahul was taken to the hospital. The doctor treated him and he became conscious. Rahul was shocked when the doctor told him how Tim saved him from the water. Rahul hugged Tim. The doctor said, “See, the dog that you hated has saved

you". Rahul said, "He is not just a dog, he is my friend Tim. Come Tim, who wants to chase me". Tim barked. And from that day, Rahul and Tim became the "best friends forever". (BFF)

Moral: A dog is a man's best friend.

PLANTS AND MODIFICATION- A NARRATIVE

(The narrative is an idea conceived by Lakshyajay to make things easier to understand, where he imagines himself to be the object narrated)

I can live without you, but you cannot live without me. Who am I? Yes, I am a plant. We are found 80% in water. We also have adaptations and make our own food. I am a leaf. I have a thing called chlorophyll inside me and it makes the food for me. We inhale carbon-di-oxide and exhale oxygen. So imagine, if we are not there, how will you survive?

Do you know potato and carrot? I have a story about a carrot.

One day Ravi and Rahul were talking. Ravi said, "Do you have carrots?" Rahul said, "Yes I have some

modified roots." Ravi said, "I don't eat roots". Rahul said, "What do you think carrots are?" I hope you have learnt from this story that carrots are modified roots. Now what's a modified root? I told you earlier that we plants have something called adaptations. For example, I am a cactus and I have modified leaves. I am found in deserts where water is very scarce. I have an adaptation, which helps me to survive in deserts. My adaptation is that I can store water in my leaves. Therefore, I have modified leaves. Did you understand? Did you like it??

I have much more to tell you, but! My gardener is coming to give me some water!!!

IT HAPPENED TO ME. EPISODE II
(The school bus incident)

(These are real life incidents, which Lakshyajay faced at various moments of his life. Through this series, he had noted down the incidents, which made an impression in his mind. The idea of writing down the incidents came from the magazine Tinkle, which he reads a lot.)

One day I was sitting in my school bus to return home. It was raining heavily. The school bus was getting delayed due to some reasons. Usually my father picks me up from the bus stop near his office from the bus, and drops me home. My father's office is very near to my home. He has two assistants in his office. One of the assistants saw a school bus entering the campus. He thought it was my school bus and informed father. Actually, it was not. As my father was busy in a meeting with a doctor, he asked his other assistant, whose name was Rajarshi to go down and wait at the dropping point, to collect me from the bus and drop me to my home. Rajarshi uncle went out accordingly. But he did not see the school bus as my school bus actually did not come. Meanwhile my

father's meeting was over. It was quite some time and Rajarshi had not returned to the office. So my father went down to the bus stop and to his astonishment Rajarshi uncle was not there. He rang home and found out that I had not reached home too. He was worried.

Meanwhile, I was still in my school bus at my school and saw Rajarshi uncle. He called me. I thought he will take me home in an auto as the bus was getting too late. My friend Manish asked me who he was. I told him the uncle works in my father's office. However, Rajarshi uncle did not take me in an auto; he made me walk in the rain till my father's office. My father was getting angry and worried, as I had still not reached his office or home. He called Rajarshi uncle. No answer. Father got more worried. Finally, Rajarshi uncle entered my father's hospital along with me. My father asked him where he was. Rajarshi uncle told him that he had gone to the school to collect me. Father got really angry and asked him as to why he did not inform father about it. Then father came to know that Rajarshi uncle made me walk all the way. Father got more angry and asked uncle as to why he did not bring me in an auto. Then he asked Rajarshi

uncle for his umbrella so that he could drop me home. He then took me to home and returned to the office.

My mother burst out in laughter when I told her about the incident. Even today, I find it very funny when I think about the incident, as to how the entire mix up created so much confusion.

THE INVISIBLE SUIT------ DOES IT REALLY EXIST

(The idea of prologue, epilogue is the result of reading a lots of books and a wish to apply it to his own story)

Prologue

Mohit told Dinesh, "Let's go. They wore an invisible suit. An invisible suit?? How did they get it and from where?? Okay let us move backwards…

The Story

One day Mohit and Dinesh went to a forest. They came across a house. They went inside and saw a man sleeping. They saw two good looking suits and wore them. Suddenly the man woke up! Dinesh said, "Sorry, we are not thieves, we just tried the clothes on, Please do not call the police!" The man said, "Whose voice is this? Who wore my suits?" Mohit asked in surprise, "You cannot see us?" The man said "No". Hearing this both of them gasped and ran out of the house. "Nobody can see us", exclaimed Mohit, "We

have become invisible by wearing these suits, but we can see each other. This is magical". They returned to their homes and slept. That is how they got the invisible suits.

Next morning, Dinesh asked Mohit, "What shall we do with these suits?" Mohit said, "Let's play a prank on Suresh, Let's go…" and the story continues

They went to Suresh's home. When they knocked at the door of Suresh's house, Suresh opened it. Suresh called out, "Hey guys! How come?" Mohit gasped. "Can you see us?" asked Dinesh. "Of course I can, why not" replied Suresh. "Come and have some tea." Mohit said, "No thanks, we will leave now."

They came back to their home. Mohit said, "What now, this suit is not working." "Let us exchange the suits", said Dinesh. "Then it might work". "It won't work", said Mohit. Dinesh said," Let's try it buddy". They exchanged their suits. Mohit said, "I think it's working". "Yes", said Dinesh. Mohit said, "Let's go and have some ice cream without paying any money." They both went to the ice cream vendor. As they tried to open the ice cream box, the ice cream

vendor shouted, "Hey! What are you doing, you naughty boys?" Mohit said, "Can you see us?" "Am I Blind", said the ice cream vendor, "Of course I can see you". They said, "Sorry uncle, there was a misunderstanding". And they rushed back home.

Dinesh said "Mohit, let's go to that creepy forest house and return the suits". They rushed to the forest. Mohit saw the man sleeping. "Wake up", shouted Mohit. The man woke up. "Who's there?" the man asked. They told the man everything. "Are these suits invisible?"asked Dinesh

The man replied, "No". Mohit asked, "Then why didn't you see us yesterday, when we wore the suits?" The man replied, "I am blind, that's why I could not see you yesterday". Mohit and Dinesh understood the whole thing and said sheepishly, "Sorry uncle, we stole your suits. Please take them back."

Dinesh and Mohit returned the suits and came back home.

Epilogue:

Dinesh and Mohit slept on their beds. At around midnight, someone knocked on their door. Dinesh opened it. He screamed loudly and fell down, because he saw a ghost. The ghost pulled out his mask, and guess who it was. It was Suresh! "How was the prank?" asked Suresh.

FEELINGS OF A TREE….. A WRITE UP ON WORLD ENVIRONMENT DAY

(Whenever we give a topic to him, Lakshyajay comes up with an innovative idea to imagine himself as the object on which he writes.)

Hello friends. Do you know who I am? No, I am not a human, I am a tree! Yesterday some woodcutters came and killed my friends. Now I have nobody around me, to whom I can talk. I am bored.

Everyone in the world knows that cutting trees is not good. Some people even write about it and many people including woodcutters read about it. But, who cares! Who cares! Everyone thinks that monkeys are bad species because it roams around the cities and steal food. But, that is only

because of humans. They cut down trees and that is why monkeys cannot stay in the forests and come down to the cities in search of food.

The human species is worse than the animal species, because humans go to the forests and kill them. Just wonder? If the animals come every day to the cities to eat humans, how many humans will be alive in the next century? Not even one!

Many species of trees are gone from our earth. My species (I am an Oak tree) also will disappear someday. We can give our life for humans, but what can they give us. Nothing!!

It was good for us in older days, humans used to sing songs to us, we were happy. But now, I don't know if in my life I can ever hear a song. The last words to you from me are: humans, you don't know, but for every tree, animal, bird, reptile and insect you are the worst species in the whole earth.

Please, don't cut trees and don't hunt animals. I don't know if you care about us or not, but, if you do care, spread this message to everyone

A REVIEW ON TOM SWIFT AND HIS SKY RACER

(The first review for a book, which he read.)

TOM SWIFT AND HIS SKY RACER OR, THE QUICKEST FLIGHT ON RECORD
BY
Victor Appleton

I read a book named Tom Swift and his sky racer, or the quickest flight on record. I will tell you how I felt when I read this book. Tom Swift is an inventor who made many things like airships, submarine, electric runabout, electric rifle etc. He lives with his father, Barton Swift in the town of Shipton, New York State. In this book, he made a sky racer named Humming Bird. There was a man named Mr. Gunmore who told him to make a sky racer and compete for the quickest flight on record. The prize money was 10,000 dollars.

After that, Mr. Swift became ill and the plans to make his sky racer remained unfilled. Tom Swift was worried. He made new plans and started building a sky racer. He faced many problems, like someone trying to destroy his sky racer and when he went to

save it, he got hurt. Another problem was that Andy Foger, his enemy tried to burn his sky racer and his father's health became worse. Finally, he made the sky racer and won the race.

I loved this book very much. I liked the feelings Tom had for his father. He gave love and respect to his father. I also loved his invention and I also liked the name Humming Bird. And the best thing is when he was racing, the wireless outfit, one of his inventions buzzed and he got to know that his father became unconscious but his last words to him were "Win the race, Tom." And he won the race. His father survived after that. I want to tell everyone that read this book and all the other books in the series Tom Swift which is written by Victor Appleton.

A MESSAGE FROM CORONA VIRUS AM I A MURDERER OR A REFORMER.

(A surprise by Lakshyajay, when he wrote about how he felt about Corona…)

Scientists believe that I am a virus. Not only scientists but also everyone thinks that I am a virus. Everyone is scared of me thinking that I will kill them. Everyone thinks that I will spread into their bodies, there will be cries of terror, the earth will have no living beings. Yes, I'll do these things. It's my nature, I can't help it.

But, do you think I like to kill? Do you think I like to hear the cries of terror? Do you think I am a murderer? The answer to all these questions is NO. I am not a murderer. What I want is a new earth. When I did not exist, you were crowding the streets. You created lots

of nuisance. You did not follow hygiene.

Just think of any family. The father of the family was so busy that he did not have time to talk to his family. Mom is always busy and does not have time to play with her son or daughter. The children: their parents made them join tuition classes, so that they do not play in the house.

But I want exactly the opposite. When I came, the father and mother now have time to spend with their family. The family life has changed. Some families do not like this change, because they want to roam around. I do not like it. Everyone should like this change. That is what I want: not deaths.

Now I think you know what I want. I want to create a new earth, which is peaceful. The earth should be clean. Trees should not live because of humans; rather humans should live for trees. That is what I want. Now who thinks I am a murderer, and I like to kill?

I want to create a new earth: a new life for everyone. Who am I? A killer or a common man? I know what you are thinking right now. You are thinking that when I create the new earth, I will disappear and after that you will destroy my new earth. But, beware, I will never disappear. My eyes will still be on you. If you start your old earth, then I will start attacking again, and you will hear the cries of terror once again.

Ha ha ha! And one more thing, this message is not only for you. Tell everyone what I want. If my message is spread like wildfire, then only I can succeed in my mission.

IT HAPPENED TO ME EPISODE III
The Kidnapers

(The innocent thoughts of the pure mind, fantasies roam galore)

I along with my mom, dad and uncle: my dad's friend, aunt and their son went for a trip to Bogibeel. It is the famous and long bridge in Assam and is near Dibrugarh. On the way, we stopped in a park called Padumoni for having our lunch.

It was in this park where the incident happened. After having lunch, I asked Mom, if we (Me and my cousin) could go to the bridge located in the park. That does not mean that I was old enough to roam around on my own, but my mom said it was safe and anyway I had my cousin too along with me.

Off we went to the bridge, and when we reached there, we saw that the bridge was old and half-broken. But it

was also not so broken that we could not walk on it. There were two men there. One of them called out, “Hey young boys, come, I will click some photos. You can cross the bridge, come hurry up.” We thought that they were kidnappers and started running without stopping for breath. We shouted on the way, “Kidnappers, help us”. But nobody even looked at us. We were running and when we looked back, we saw the kidnappers were still behind us.

After running a long way, we suddenly realized that we were not running the right way. Where were our parents? We looked everywhere and finally saw where our parents were. But we were far ahead from where our parents were. We had to make a U-turn. The kidnappers were not there anymore and we made it to our parents. We told them everything. Dad said, “Wait, I will go and see those kidnappers.

We went there, but there was nobody there. Perhaps they are gone, I said. “Perhaps you mistook those innocent people for kidnappers”, dad said. “I think they really wanted to click your photos. I replied, “But why were they chasing us then?” Dad replied, “Maybe it was someone else who was wearing similar looking clothes and going their own way. Anyway, how could they get in the park through the security gate without the security guards knowing that they were kidnappers? And how would they get out of here?

The it became clear that it our mistake, and we continued playing for some more time, before finally proceeding towards Bogibeel, and that friends is another story. So Goodbye for now.

THE ELEPHANT CITY

(A fantasy story with a moral, maybe the news of innocent elephants being maltreated by human has made a mark in his young mind. He tries to portray it in his own way, something we adults too should think..)

There were 2 explorers, named Rohit and Rajiv. One day they decided to go to a forest to explore. The forest was dangerous, with many wild and ferocious animals. And some people also said that it was a forbidden forest. Rohit and Rajiv ate some fritters and French fries before starting on their exploration. When they reached the forest, Rohit saw a beautiful waterfall. "Wow! That's so beautiful,"said Rohit. "It's a wonder why people say that it's a forbidden forest."

Rajiv went near the waterfall and saw a caterpillar on a twig. He touched it and the waterfall disappeared. There was a hidden door at the place from where the water was flowing. Rohit said "Oh my god! That's quite a place to explore! Let's go in!" They went in and before them was a place where elephants were talking like them, walking like them, driving cars like

them, buying things like them and in a big board there was written " ELEPHANT CITY".

An elephant came to them and said "Welcome to ELEPHANT CITY.""Please don't harm us", said Rajiv. "No I won't," said the elephant. "My name is Bhola". "Do you have some food?" asked Rajiv. "Yes I have" replied Bhola. They ate some sandwiches, bacon and steak. "Any places to visit?" asked Rohit. "Yes", replied Bhola. "There is the No Gravity Room, the Creepville Haunted House, Dream Island, Pirate Island and Treasure Island." They visited the places. And I can't say how much they liked the No Gravity Room. They flew on helicopters and they liked the place very much.

Then an elephant named Raju came to them and informed them that the king wanted to meet them. Bhola took them to the king. The king welcomed Rohit and Rajiv and said, "How do you like our place?" "It's wonderful", said Rohit and Rajiv together.

Then Rajiv asked the king, "Why are you living here? Don't you like the forest?"

The king was astonished. He replied, "I will tell you the reason. The reason is that, we loved the forests a lot. But nowadays, people have started cutting down the forests and they also hunt us and kill us down for our tusks. So we had no other option but to make a world of our own. A world where we can live in peace away from the humans. But the problem is if the humans come to know of our land, then they will come here too and kill us. That is why we built our city behind the waterfalls. No one will notice us."

The king continued, "But now that you have discovered our land, please don't go and tell others about this. Otherwise people will come here and again kill us. Will you promise us that you will keep this journey a secret and never say a word of it to anyone else?

Rohit and Rajiv said, "O King, we promise you that we will never share his secret. We, on behalf of all human beings say sorry to you for the troubles we caused you. Actually you are really very good, and we don't need to be afraid of you, you are kind gentle and caring. We promise you that your land will always remain safe."

Rohit and Rajiv then wished the king bye and thanked Bhola for the hospitality. They left the city and never told a word about it to anyone. And till today, once in a week they visit the elephant city, but no one knows which forest it is or where the waterfall is.

WHY I LOVE READING BOOKS.

(A simple and short narration of why he loves books and also what he thinks about books)

Today I want to share a secret with you all. Do you know who my best friend is? Well I do have friends in my school, but my best friend is Books. Why? Because books have everything. It has knowledge, stories, novels etc. But the question is why I love reading books. Let's know the answer

Books help us in many ways. If we read books, we can become doctors, engineers or any other profession we like. We can pass in exams and become intelligent if we read knowledge books. We can

have good habits and good behaviour if we read moral stories. And what about novels? We can get many ideas from novels like Sherlock Holmes and Hardy Boys if we want to become detectives. We can also get inspiration to do great things by reading life stories of great persons.

Books are best friends because they always keep your company. Friends can fight with us but books will never fight. Friends may leave us in times of need, but books never will. Friends may make us sad, but books always make us happy. In the recent time of lockdown, I did not have friends, but books made sure I was never lonely. That is why I love books. We can buy toys, but they will break, but a book will always remain with me, and I can read it after many days also.

Just like friends, we should also take care of our books. We should keep our books safely. We should not tear the pages or write something on it. We should keep it in a safe place after reading it. Even if we do not need a book, we should not tear it or throw it way, because we can donate it to some library, so that some other people can read it and gather knowledge.

We should not read books in the dark, because it will harm our eyes. We should also not read it lying down.

There are some people in the world who loves every

kind of books. And there are some people who start screaming at the name of books. I am the first type. I love books. I believe that when we read books, we should get inside the book. We should learn to feel and experience what the book says.

My last word to everyone is that "Forget the mobiles, televisions, PCs and go the interesting world of books.

IT HAPPENED TO ME EPISODE IV (SIGHTING OF THE TIGER)

(Lakshyajay's first trip to a wildlife sanctuary and experience of a forest. Incidentally, he even sighted tigers which is considered a rarity in Kaziranga)

Once my dad, mom and I went to visit my father's friend Deepak Khura (Uncle) at Melamora. He has a beautiful changghar named Meluha. There are lot of interesting things in Meluha. It was a beautiful and interesting place full of antique things.

Deepak khura took us on an interesting trip. Guess where we went? It was Kaziranga (a wild life sanctuary famous for the one-horned rhinos in Assam). We took a Jeep Safari. We had binoculars with us to see the distant things. It was such a pleasant journey and my father made videos on his

mobile phone. We saw rhinos, deer, elephants, bisons, and many birds in the trip. We also saw some beautiful birds including a very big owl. We also saw many trees.

As the trip was going to end, we were hoping to see a tiger. But Deepak Khura as well the driver and the guard said that it was very rare to see tigers and it was impossible to see the tiger at the end of the j journey, as tigers usually stay only in deep forest. I was feeling very sad that I could not see a tiger.

Then suddenly, a tiger crossed our path. The driver stopped the vehicle and told us to be silent. My father heard a rustling sound behind him and also a sort of growl. We turned back to see what it was and lo! Right behind us in the bushes was a tigress with her two cubs. The tigress was looking at us with big eyes. It was very dangerous as she was protecting her kids.

The tigress was looking at us and was ready to pounce at us. And then suddenly one more tiger jumped up from the bush and believe me it was a big one. However, the tigress might have understood that we were not going to harm her or her cubs, and she slowly went away with her cubs. And all this happened just some six feet away from where we were sitting.

We were shocked for some time. My father asked the guard as to why he did not take any action like blank firing his gun to protect us. However, the guards said

that he had never experienced such a situation or seen a tiger before, and he forgot what to do.

We waited for some time fearfully, and when we were sure that there no more tigers, the driver started the vehicle and he moved away.

This was the most scariest and terrifying incident of my life, where I got to see a tiger with cubs at just few feet away from us. I still wonder what would have happened if the tigress pounced on us.

THE DOG EATER

(A mystery-solving story... Maybe the result of the inquisitiveness mind and effect of reading Sherlock Holmes)

One day Shyam was feeding a piece of bread to his dog named Lightning. He saw a red car coming. "Hey Shyam!" shouted the man in the car. "Where's Jaguar? Oh! That's Lightning" Jaguar was also Shyam's dog. "Mr. Manish Malhotra!" said Shyam. "Jaguar is in my bungalow. Come and meet him." Mr. Malhotra entered the bungalow of Shyam. "Jaguar, where are you", shouted Shyam. However, Jaguar was not there. Shyam was worried. He said, "Where has Jaguar gone? Let us Search for him in his favourite place, the jungle. He must have gone there. There are no wild beasts there." And they went out to search Jaguar in the forest. But Jaguar was nowhere to be found. And when they returned, they found out that Lightning was missing too.

Many dogs were found to be missing in the city. The newspapers were filled with news of lost dogs. Shyam's family consisted of his wife and two children

Mohan and Piya. The day when Lightning and Jaguar were stolen, Mohan and Piya were in the school.

Two days later, when Mohan and Piya were returning from the school, they saw a big crowd. In the middle of the crowd, there was a man wearing some funny looking goggles. He was telling the crowd, "Friends, you know that there are many dogs reported missing in the city. Do you have any idea who is stealing them? The DOG EATER. I saw the dog eater in the forest nearby, when I went there for some work. I have come to know that the dog eater is a cannibal. He eats human flesh too. So please be careful to not leave your dogs alone and yeah do not go to the forest. I have proof. See this picture, the dog eater is eating a dog." Everyone was shocked.

Mohan and Piya returned home. "Piya" said Mohan, "That man was talking about the monster, wasn't he? But I don't believe it. The man was saying he saw the dog eater, but how can he be sure that the dog eater eats humans too? And when Jaguar was stolen, Dad and Malhotra uncle went to search for Jaguar in the forest. How is it possible that they did

not see any dog eater there?" Piya too agreed, "Yes, I think so. Tomorrow we will go there after school. But we can't go to the forest alone. We will ask Suraj also to come with us." "Yes", said Mohan.

The next day, they went to school. They met Suraj and told him about their plan. After school, they went to the forest where the dog eater lives. And surprisingly, they saw the Man who was talking about the dog eater, discussing something with Mr. Malhotra, two ladies and some more people. There were some white packets near them. "Drugs", shouted Mohan Piya and Suraj. "They are smuggling drugs." Mr. Malhotra heard them. "Hey! Stop! You meddling kids." The man who said about the doge eater shouted, "Go and get them". Mr. Malhotra ran towards the kids. They also ran. Mr. Malhotra caught Suraj and Piya. But, Mohan could manage to escape and reached home. But his parents were not there. "Oh no" he cried loudly. "I forgot that Mom and Dad have gone to the mall. There is no phone here, and I don't know the way to the police station."

He began to think what to do. "Oh, Idea" said Mohan. He rushed to the forest after recording something in a recorder. Meanwhile, Suraj and Piya were both tied and then they saw the dog eater. They were surprised to see that the dog eater was actually a man in the costume of a monster. All the missing dogs including Jaguar and Lightning were locked in a cage. Just then, everyone heard a loud voice. "Drug Smugglers, your game is over. I am Mohan, come and

fight with me." All the smugglers went towards the voice. Suraj and Piya saw Mohan. Mohan said, "That's my voice in the recorder". He untied them. Piya said, "That's the master key, unlock the dogs quickly." Mohan quickly unlocked all the dogs and the dogs attacked the smugglers. There was a phone in the table. Mohan dialled the police station and his dad, and soon the police arrived and arrested the smugglers.

Shyam too arrived at the spot and was surprised to see his friend Mr. Malhotra there. He asked Malhotra, "Malhotra, you are also involved in this smuggling business. Mr. Malhotra said, "Shyam, I will tell you what happened. There is nothing called a dog eater. One day, I was approached by the boss of this gang and they offered me five lakhs rupees, if I helped them steal some dogs. I became greedy and agreed to help them. That is how Jaguar was stolen, when I kept you busy in talks outside your house. Then when we went to the forest to look for Jaguar, Lightning was stolen. We then spread the rumour that there was dog eater in the forest who was also a cannibal. Moreover, we also planned to use the dogs to smuggle the drugs, by tying drugs inside their collars. Our plan was going on smoothly until these meddling kids got us."

Mohan, Piya and Suraj were given a bravery award by the police and their parents were proud of them. Mr. Malhotra and others were sentenced to prison for eleven years.

ROHAN'S ANGER

(A story depicting the ill effects of anger, and how it harms one)

Rohan at night asked his mother if she could make him some sandwiches for tiffin instead of chapattis. Mother agreed. The next day Mohan went to school and eagerly waited for recess. In the recess time, he went to have his tiffin with his friends, Ravi, Pinky and Arjun, in the school playground. When he reached there he opened his tiffin box, and instead of sandwiches, there were chapattis.

"What happenedRohan?" asked Arjun. "You were boasting yesterday that you will bring sandwiches. See I brought pastries.' Rohan was very angry. He threw his tiffin to the ground and went to class. "Kids did you learn for today's test?" asked the teacher. "Answer these questions". Rohan was very angry and wrote the answers wrongly even though he knew the right answers.

When he came home, he threw his bag on the sofa, his shoes on the bed and clothes on the floor. "Why are you behaving like this?" asked his mother. "Why did you give me chapattis and not sandwiches?" His mother said, "Oh, sorry Rohan, by mistake I gave your sandwiches to your dad and his chapattis to you. Come and eat lunch." "I will not eat lunch today", shouted Rohan and locked himself in his room.

Some hours passed. Rohan was hungry but he did not eat. In the evening Rohan's mother went to his room. The door was locked. "Rohan, open the door", said his mother. No answer came. She called Rohan's father and Rohan's father forced the door open. They saw Rohan lying unconscious on the floor. They took him to the hospital.

The doctor told Rohan's parent that he became unconscious due to hunger. "He must have not eaten food for a long time," the doctor said. His mother gave Rohan some food.

"What happened Mother?" asked Rohan. "Why am I

here?" His parents told Rohan the whole incident. Rohan realised his mistake and said, "Sorry Mom, Sorry Dad, I will try to control my anger from now and will never stay without food."

Rohan had learnt his lesson. We should all try to control our anger because it is very harmful for us.

THE THREE WISHES

(A fantasy story, which Lakshyajay wrote. The story depicts, how innocent children are, which is clear on the three wishes made at the end of the story.)

Amar was an archaeologist. He studied stones. One day he went to a forest with Raj, Amit, Mohan and Suraj, his friends. There they started picnicking. "Guys", Amar said, "I am just going to explore this place, and you guys enjoy the burgers, but keep one for me too." And Amar set out to explore. He saw a cave behind some bushes and went in. After going deep inside the cave, he found coals and some precious stones. I am doing a treasure hunter's job and not mine, but it's fun, thought Amar. He extracted some of the precious stones and put them in his back pack, and suddenly a boulder rolled in towards him. He started running to save himself. At last he saw a door. Without thinking, he opened the large door and entered inside to save himself from the boulder. "What"! He gasped. There were many sculptures of gold, precious stones, and some gold too. Amar stuffed some of them in his bag and then saw another door. He opened the door and entered

inside. He saw it was an old room. There were broken chandeliers and also some broken chairs etc. There were cobwebs everywhere. "Oh, this place is becoming very scary; I should get out of here before it is too late. I should now get out of here." Amar thought and after a long search, he somehow came out the cave.

It was still not too dark. He found his friends. "Where were you? See its already evening. We were starting to get worried" asked his friends. "Let's go to my house, I will tell you everything there", said Amar. "What's there in that bag?" asked Suraj. "Let's go to my home, I will tell you everything there in detail. I am feeling very tired" Amar yawned and said.

After reaching Amar's home, he narrated everything to his friends. "What?" said Raj, "Tell me you are joking, I don't believe this?" "I have proof", said Amar. He opened the bag and showed them the precious stones and gold. "Whoa" said Amit, "I want to see that place. Will you take me there tomorrow?" "No!" exclaimed Suraj, "remember the boulder; it must have been thrown by someone. I am scared that

we might get hurt". "Hey! Don't say such things, the boulder might have moved when I tried to extract the stones from the walls" said Amar. So it was decided that next morning they will go the cave and explore. Amar's friends returned to their homes.

Amar then took out the precious stones and found a peculiar stone. He researched it and found out that the stone was around 1000 years old. He tried to clean it with a cloth and saw blue smoke coming out of it. And then he saw a Genie. "What?" cried Amar? "Is this thing a genie? No it can't be. Genies do not have legs! And this thing has legs!" Amar realized that he had seen the strange man before. He rushed to his library and brought out a book named "The history of the olden Times". He turned its pages hurriedly. Some of the pages were dirty and old and some were torn too. He turned to page no. 63, looked at it and looked at the man. "Sir Oliver IX", shouted Amar. The man was the king Sir Oliver IX. "What a great discovery", shouted Amar in delight. "I am Amar, Sir,

You are still alive! I thought you were dead a long time ago!" "No", said Sir Oliver IX. Amar asked "Then how are you alive. How are you trapped in this stone?" Sir Oliver took a deep breath and said, "Many centuries ago, I was a king and lived happily. I had all the wealth, but money was not very important for me. I wanted to be immortal and I called many wizards, witches and magicians, but no one could make me immortal. One day my friend told me that there was a very powerful wizard, who could solve my problem. So I set out on Hunter, my horse and went out looking for the wizard. He told me that he could solve my problem. But, only on one condition. I will have to give him my entire wealth and the palace. I shouted, Is it immortality or a curse you are giving me. He told me that why should I be worried, after becoming immortal, I can snatch anyone's wealth. No one could kill me."

"But by them I had snatched the potion forcefully and drank it. I became immortal. The wizard was very angry. He could not kill me, so he cursed me that I will turn into a stone, and I was trapped inside this stone. He said that I can be free only if someone rubs the stone. I will be free, but I have to be the slave of that person. I can get rid of the curse and attain freedom of my soul, only if I fulfil three wishes of my master and the master tells me to break the stone. But if my master does not break the stone, I will turn into the stone again and will have to wait for a new master. He also put all my wealth in the cave with his magic. This was my story. Now tell me your three wishes, so

that I can fulfil them".

Sir Oliver IX continued, "Master, you can only fulfil three wishes, so think wisely before you make a wish". Amar said, "Listen, my wishes may seem a little awkward. But I want you to fulfil them. My first wish is that, I want you to close the mouth of the cave from where I found you. My second wish is that you make my friends forget everything about what happened today and my third wish is that you break the stone."

Sir Oliver asked, "May I ask you master why did you ask for these awkward wishes instead of wealth etc.?"

Amar replied, "The reason for the first wish is, if that cave is spotted, then people will start fighting for the gold and precious stones inside the cave. But the things actually belong to you, don't they?" "Yes", said Sir Oliver. "So I don't won't your things to be stolen". "The reason for the second wish is that my friends should not remember anything, otherwise they will try to find out about the cave and loot it. And the reason for my last wish is that I want you to be free. You will not turn into a stone anymore."

Sir Oliver granted his wishes and said, "Thank you Amar, you have a golden heart. I wish all the best for you and will pray for your success always.

Saying this Sir Oliver IX slowly disappeared in a puff of smoke. However, Amar still feels that Sir Oliver IX

is always near him. Is it because Sir Oliver IX drank the immortality potion?

THE PROTECTOR OF THE FORESTS

(A long story presented chapter wise, another innovation. The story once again depicts his love for nature and his intense wish for preserving nature at all costs)

Chapter I: Raj's Vacation

There was a boy named Raj. He was very adventurous. He always studied very well. His holidays were coming and his parents told him that they would take him to his grandma's house. He like Grandma's house because it was near a forest and he loved animals a lot. They packed and went to grandma's house by flight.

Chapter II: The great forest

Raj reached his grandma's house. "Raj", cried his grandma in delight. "My sweetheart, come here". Raj hugged his grandma and they went inside the home. While eating lunch Raj said, "Grandma, Can I go the jungle nearby. I love jungles and the animals." "No, you cannot go alone," said Raj's mom. "Let him go and explore, he is big enough now", said grandma.

"Raj, you can go tomorrow". Raj got ready to go to the jungle the next day.

Chapter III: The friendly tiger.

Raj went to the forest. The birds were singing. The weather was pleasant. It was a good day for a walk in the jungle. Everything was going right until Raj heard a growl. Raj looked around and saw a tiger. The tiger came near Raj. Raj was scared. But then he saw that there was a thorn in the tiger's foot and it was limping. Raj gathered courage and took out the thorn. The tiger growled, but it did not do any harm to Raj. It licked Raj's hands. "Whoa! I have a tiger as a friend now," said Raj. "I should name it, Hmmm I will call it Tig. How do you like the name Tig?" Raj asked the tiger. The tiger seemed to like the name and from then on Raj called the tiger "Tig".

Chapter IV: The cave of the bear.

One day Raj went to the forest and called Tig. "Tig" shouted Raj. Tig came out from the bushes and licked Raj's hand. Raj played with Tig. As usual, they walked in the forest and saw a cave. "Wow"! Said Raj, "Come Tig, let's go into the cave. They went inside the cave and saw a bear sleeping. "Better not to wake him up", said Raj slowly. When they were coming out of the cave, Raj stepped on a branch and made a crackling sound. The sound woke up the bear. The bear was very ferocious. It was growling and going to attack Raj. But Tig jumped in front of Raj and growled loudly. The bear also growled. The two animals kept growling for some time, and finally the

bear went to sleep again. Raj felt that both the animals were talking something in their own language.

Chapter V: The poachers

Some days after the bear incident, it was time for Raj to return home. His grandma said, "Raj, go to the forest and play as much as you can." Raj rushed to the forest and called Tig. "Tig", said Raj, "Today is my last day here. I will come next year, don't feel bad". Tig moaned. Raj rubbed Tig on his forehead. Just then, they heard a gunshot. Raj said, "Tig, go and hide behind those bushes, quick, NOW! Raj climbed a tree and looked down. He saw some men with guns who looked like poachers.

"Ranjit boss" said one of the poachers. "What do you think we should catch today?" "Maybe a tiger", said another one. "Yes", said another one, whom Raj thought to be Ranjit, the boss of the gang. "Very good Mangal, Suraj Sunny and Sunil, my orders today are to catch a tiger." Just then, the branch on which Raj was sitting broke and he fell down.

Chapter VI: Prisoner

Mangal said, "What fell down?" He looked around and saw Raj. "Hey kid, why are you here?" Ranjit the boss shouted, "Hey catch him, he may call theforest guards." "You will be spotted if you fire a gun. You were lucky that the first shot was not heard by the guards." Raj said. "He is right boss", said Mangal. As they were busy discussing, Raj suddenly broke free and started running. The poachers chased Raj. Suddenly Raj tripped over a stone and fell down. The poachers caught him and tied him. Raj was now a prisoner of the poachers.

Chapter VII: Will Raj die?

"What should be done with this boy, Boss", asked Sunny. Ranjit replied, "I think we should throw him in the river which is inside the forest?" Raj burst out into tears and pleaded, "No, I can't swim, please don't throw me in the river. I do not want to die. Please let me go."

Meanwhile Raj's parents and grandma were looking for Raj, as it was very late. They were very worried. They came down to the forest to look for him. As they entered the forest, Tig suddenly came out in front of them. Tig growled. "Oh my God," said Raj's father, "That's a tiger? Where in the world is Raj?" Raj's father did not know that Tig was Raj's friend and was about to shoot Tig. Then a voice came, "Dad Stop, Don't shoot him. He is my friend." It was Raj. Tig jumped on Raj and licked him. His parents and

grandma hugged him. "What happened? Why is this tiger licking you?" asked Grandma.

Chapter VIII: Raj narrates the story.

Raj began narrating the story. All about his friendship with Tig, the incident about the bear's cave, the poachers and how he was made a prisoner. He then narrated how he escaped from the poachers and what happened next.

"The poacher took me to the river and untied my hands. They made fun of me and threw me into the river, thinking I would drown. However, I had lied to them and they did not know that I was a good swimmer. I started to swim, but the poachers also jumped into the river and chased me. Finally, they caught me. Ranjit pointed a gun to my head. I was sure that this was my end. I closed my eyes." Raj said. "What happened after that?" asked grandma. Raj continued, "Just then a man came swinging from the trees and kicked Sunny. He punched Ranjit and gave a flying kick to him. Then he mumbled something and at once a bear, a tiger and some other animals came out from the bushes and killed the poachers. The man gave me a handshake. He said, 'I am Bhola, the protector of the jungle. My grandfather, Boopa Bholenath Das was also the protector of the jungle. I hate poachers. I know the language of the animals and can talk to them. Today a baby tiger came to me and told me about you. I immediately followed you and saw your bravery. Now let's go back to your parents, who must be worried about you.'

Raj then called Bhola who was hiding behind a tree and introduced him to his parents and grandma. Raj's parents and grandma thanked Bhola for saving Raj as well as the animals from the poachers. Raj said, ", Bhola next time, when I come here, teach me how to talk to animals so that I can talk to Tig and other animals. When I grow up, I will also like to become the protector of the jungle like you. We will see you in my next vacation. What a great adventure". Tig started moaning. "He is saying, don't go" translated Bhola. "I will come back again, Tig" said Raj, bid goodbye to Tig, Bhola, and came out of the forest.

Chapter IX: The ending

This was the beginning of Raj's adventures. Every year Raj visited Tig and Bhola. Raj learnt the language of animals from Bhola and spent most of his time talking to Tig. Sometimes Raj brought Tig to grandma's house also, of course hidden from other people. Tig liked it there with the tasty food and lying on the sofa. When Raj grew up, he became the next protector of the jungle after Bhola's death. Tig also died. But Raj is still alive and every animals in the forest, may it be the tiger, lion, elephant and every animal in the forest love him a lot. He never lets poachers enter the jungle, and here our story ends.

THE BANDORKENKUA, (A KIND OF POISONOUS NETTLE) (MONKEY TAMARIND)

(A story based on a true incident. The rubbing of the Bandor kenkua (Monkey Tamarind) incident happened with his father. When the incident was narrated to him, he made his own story using fictitious characters.)

Rajat, his wife Lata, their son Raghav and daughter Pihu were going to Rajasthan by train. It was the first train journey for Raghav and Pihu. They had a lot of luggage with them. Upon reaching the train station, they took a porter to carry their entire luggage to the train compartment. The porter said, "Sir, be careful, you have so much luggage with you. There are many thefts in this train for a long time." Rajat thanked the porter and settled down.

Nandini ghosh

As the train started in the journey, Raghav and Pihu looked out of the window and saw many huts, villages and ponds. They also had some

comics with them. At around noon, as there was nothing to do, everyone except Raghav and Pihu began sleeping. At that time, they read their comics. The train stopped at a station. "Mom, Dad", said Raghav, "Let's buy some food outside. I am starving." Lata said, "We have some food with us." "But that's for dinner", Pihu said. "There is enough food for lunch also", said Rajat. They all ate lunch. As they were taking lunch, an odd-looking man entered the compartment and sat down opposite them. The odd man wore thick looking glasses and had a frown on his forehead. It looked like he was some kind of a thief. Moreover, the man kept looking at Raghav and his family. "Look at that man, I don't think he is a good person", whispered Raghav in Pihu's ear. "I think so "whispered Pihu. "He might be a thief", "Not he might, he is a thief," whispered Raghav. They saw that their parents were also whispering something.

In the next station another man, who looked like a gentleman entered their compartment and sat on the seat opposite to them. The man started a conversation with them and they came to know that his name was Suraj; He worked in a big company and was travelling to the same station they were going. Raghav and Pihu became very friendly with Suraj, but they also kept an eye on the old man. The day passed off. As it was time to sleep, Rajat locked all the bags and lied down on his berth. Raghav and Pihu decided to keep awake to keep an eye on the old person. After some time,

they were so sleepy that they could not even open their eyes properly and they dozed off.

Suddenly Raghav heard a noise and saw a figure. It was very dark; he could not see the face. "Pihu", he whispered. Pihu woke up. They followed the figure to the toilet. Five figures were already waiting there. They were talking. While going they observed that the odd looking man was not in his berth. So they became sure that he was one of them. One of the men said, "They are still awake, I think they may have suspected you", he pointed to one of the men. Raghav and Pihu became sure that it was the odd looking man they were referring to. Raghav said, "Pihu, he is the man". The men heard them and looked at them. But they rushed back to their seats and told their mom, "Mom, some people are talking about us, one of them saw me". But by then the train had stopped at a station and their mom did not pay heed to them and said, "I will hear it later, let's go". They came out of the bogie. It was not so dark in the station. Raghav and Pihu saw that the man who looked at them was not the old man, but it was Suraj, the gentleman. The old man must have got off at some other station.

Suddenly Suraj from behind dropped something on Rajat's neck. Rajat's neck and back started itching. It was Bandor kenkua or the Monkey tamarind. Bandor kenkua or Monkey Tamarind is a plant, which causes intense itching. Suraj said, "Sir, someone has thrown Bandor kenkua on your back. You should wash it immediately with water." The other thieves also agreed. Rajat said, "Lata, pour some water on my back". "No Mom, don't" shouted Raghav and Pihu together. "Suraj uncle is a thief". They narrated the whole story. Suraj tried to escape, but Raghav chased him. While running Suraj dropped the bag of Monkey Tamarind. Raghav picked up the bag of Monkey tamarind and threw it over Suraj. Suraj sat down scratching as it began itching terribly. By that time, other people had also arrived and they caught Suraj. "Dad, do you know why I stopped you from washing your back?"askedRaghav. "Because today I read about monkey Tamarind and came to know that that the itching becomes terrible if you try to wash it off with water. So you should never try to put water if you come in contact with Bandor kenkua or Monkey Tamarind."

Everyone present praised Raghav for his prompt action and they handed over Suraj to the railway police. The railway police thanked Raghav and Pihu for nabbing Suraj, who turned out to be the leader of the gang of thieves who were looting passengers by throwing Bandor kenkua or Monkey Tamarind on people, and snatching away their belongings.

Rajat then took some medicines to get relief and they came out of the railway station. The railway police awarded Raghav and Pihu for their bravery and thus the first train journey for both of them turned out to be very adventurous and thrilling.

And Raghav and Pihu both thanked the books they read for giving them knowledge about Monkey Tamarind, which helped them to save their father from great trouble and by now,everyone, must have understood the importance of reading book. So I appeal to everyone to read books instead of wasting time on Mobiles and TV.

www.ingramcontent.com/pod-product-compliance
Lightning Source LLC
LaVergne TN
LVHW050419160726
843469LV00041B/1140

* 9 7 8 9 3 5 4 5 8 3 2 8 5 *